No More Peanuts for Ellie the Elephant

A Children's Coloring Book on Peanut Allergies

By: Christine E. Cirillo

Illustrated by: Mel Schroeder

No More Peanuts For Ellie the Elephant.
(Health Awareness Series, Book 1)

Copyright © 2017, 2020 Christine E. Cirillo

First edition published 2017. Second edition published 2020.

Cover Illustration © 2020 Mel Schroeder
Cover & Interior Design © 2020 Mel Schroeder

All rights reserved. No portion of this book may be reproduced mechanically, electronically, or by any other means, including photocopying, without written permission of the publisher.

ISBN-13: 979-8699077106

DEDICATION:

To Patrick and Lilian Kerner,

our two newest members of the family.

Ellie the Elephant lived at the zoo,

Right next to her friend
Kenny, the Kangaroo.

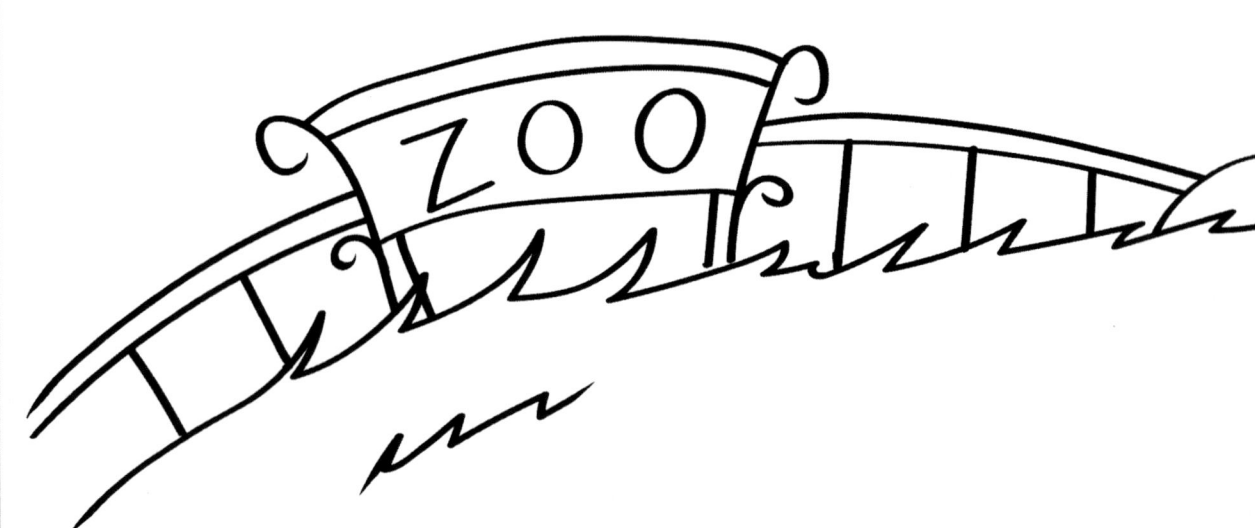

At lunch time Ellie and Kenny always ate alone,

At the "Peanut-Free Zone".

One day a little girl named Suzie came along,

She wanted to feed the elephants peanuts,

...which was very, very wrong.

Suzie gave peanuts to all the elephants at the zoo,

Even Ellie, had a peanut too...

A few minutes later,

Ellie got a very itchy rash...

which became greater and greater.

And as Ellie's reaction spread,

Her trunk and tongue became all swollen and red.

Ellie rushed to her mommy,

With a strange pain in her tummy.

Ellie's trunk started to close,

And then...

Her vet came rushing over with a **magic pen.**

The vet used all of his force,
oh my!

And swung the magic pen into
Ellie's outer thigh.

He slowly counted

1... 2... 3...

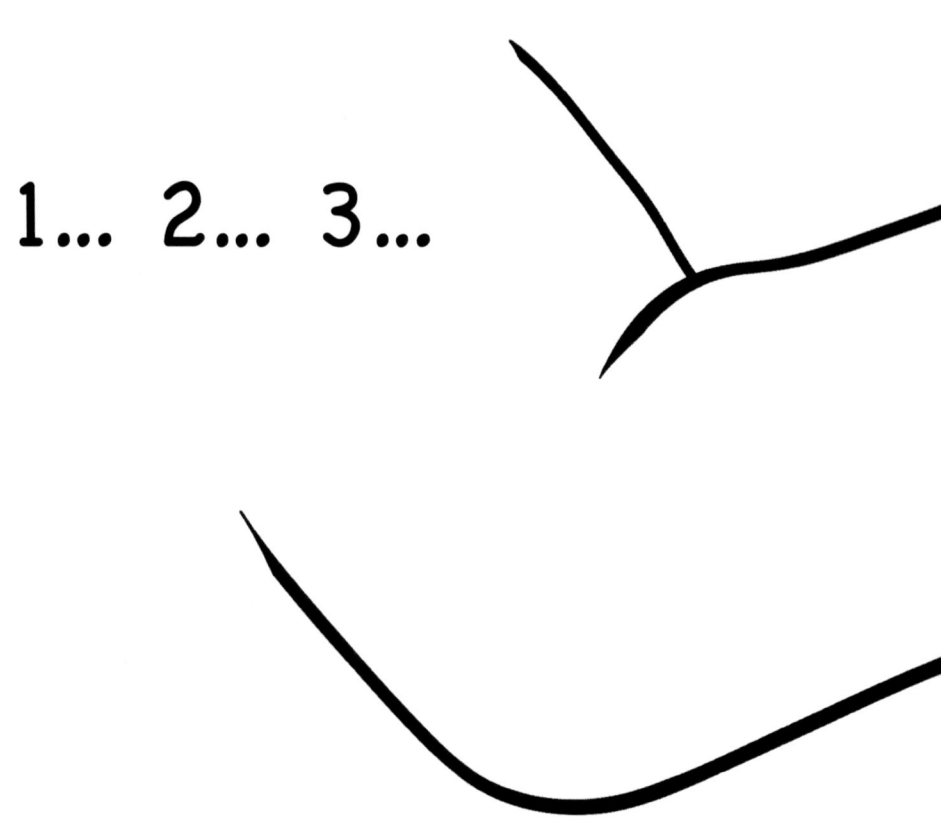

And dropped it far away from Ellie.

Ellie started feeling much, much better...

And now she knows why she can never eat a peanut again,

...or even Peanut Butter!

INFORMATION FOR PARENTS:

Peanut allergies is one of the most common food allergies. It can cause a severe, potentially life-threatening allergic reaction called <u>anaphylaxis</u>. Be alert to warning signs. For example: A child may say, "my tongue (or lips) feel tingly" after eating a certain food. This is a reason to seek medical follow-up.

Know your child's symptoms. Teach your child about his or her allergy. They are never too young to learn. Read all food labels and teach your child this habit.

At restaurants, schools, or bakeries always ask if there is any peanuts in foods or any peanut cross-contamination. Check the ingredients list on foods and look on the label for phrases like these:

- "May contain tree nuts."
- "May contain peanuts."
- "Produced on shared equipment with tree nuts or peanuts."

Inform all your child's care-givers, teachers, school nurse, friends, and their parents, of your child's allergy. This notification is very important, consider purchasing an allergy alert ID bracelet with your child's allergy listed.

Consult your child's pediatrician/physician on what medicine to administer with an allergic reaction. If an EpiPen® ("Magic Pen") is prescribed, learn how to use it, as well as all care-givers.

So what kind of "nut" is a peanut. It's not truly a nut! A peanut is actually a legume, which is in a different family from nuts: walnuts, almonds, cashews, hazelnuts, pistachio.

Signs & Symptoms...

Skin reactions (hives, redness, swelling), itching or tingling of tongue or mouth, digestive problems (stomach cramps, nausea, vomiting, diarrhea), tightening of throat, shortness of breath or wheezing (this could be anaphylaxis).

THE USE OF AN EPIPEN® IS FOR LIFE-THREATENING ANAPHYLAXIS.

YOU MUST CALL 911 IF YOUR CHILD IS HAVING AN ALLERGIC REACTION REQUIRING THE USE OF AN EPIPEN®

PLEASE NOTE: EXPIRATION DATES ON THE EPIPEN® AND REPLACE AS NEEDED. MAKE SURE ALL KEY PERSONNEL INVOLVED WITH YOUR CHILD HAVE AN EPIPEN.

Made in United States
North Haven, CT
13 September 2024

57373101R00015